Why Shouldn't I Drop Litter?

M J Knight

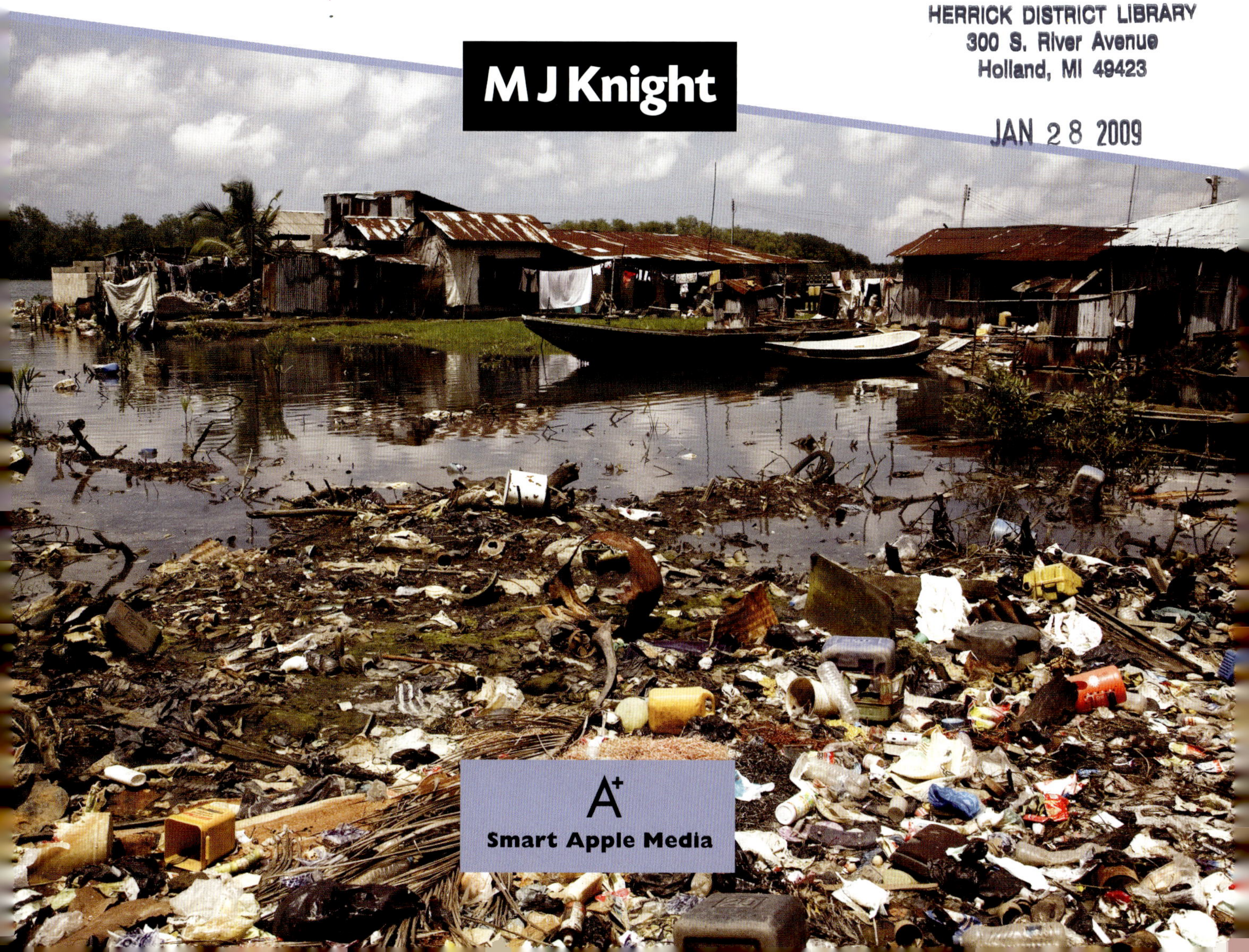

A+
Smart Apple Media

Smart Apple Media is published by Black Rabbit Books
P.O. Box 3263, Mankato, Minnesota 56002

U.S. publication copyright © 2009 Black Rabbit Books. International copyright reserved in all countries. No part of this book may be reproduced in any form without written permission from the publisher.

Printed in China

Library of Congress Cataloging-in-Publication Data

Knight, M. J. (Mary-Jane)
　Why shouldn't I drop litter? / M.J. Knight.
　p. cm. — (Smart Apple Media. One small step)
　Summary: "Facts about how litter harms the environment and practical tips for kids about how they can contribute to cleaning up their neighborhoods"—Provided by publisher.
　Includes bibliographical references and index.
　ISBN 978-1-59920-265-5 (hardcover)
　1. Litter (Trash)—Juvenile literature. I. Title.
TD813.K59 2009
363.72'8—dc22
　　　　　　　　　　　　　　　　　　　　　　　　　　2008011379

Designed by Guy Callaby
Edited by Jinny Johnson
Illustrations by Hel James
Picture research by Su Alexander

Picture acknowledgements
Title Page Ed Kashi/Corbis; 4 Tony Kurdzuk/Star Ledger/Corbis; 6 Kevin R Morris/Corbis; 7 Mika/Zefa/Corbis; 8 Getty Images; 9 Chris Jones/Corbis; 10 Kim Karpeles/Alamy; 11 FrameZero/Alamy; 12 P.Desgieux/Photocuisine/Corbis; 15 Jose Fuste Raga/Corbis; 16 Ian Goodrick/Alamy; 17 Stan Kujawa/Alamy; 19 Gideon Mendel/Corbis; 21 Ed Kashi/Corbis; 22-23 & 25 Ashley Cooper/Corbis; 27 Pat Canova/Alamy; 28 Fabrice Bettex/Alamy; 29 Jonathan Blair/Corbis; Front cover: Craig Steven Thrasher/Alamy

9 8 7 6 5 4 3 2 1

Contents

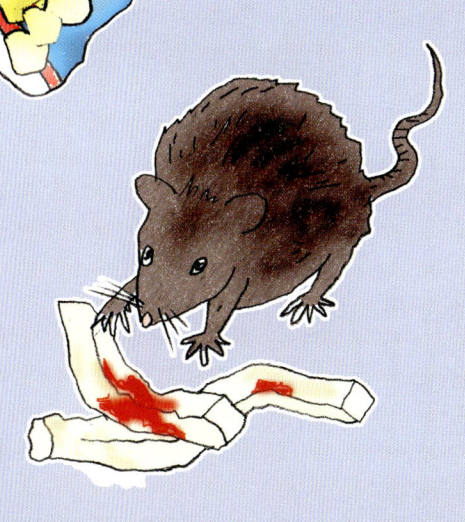

4 A Whole Lot of Litter
6 What Is Litter?
8 Litter in the Streets
10 Cleaning the Streets
12 Packaging and Fast Food
14 What Do We Throw Away at Home?
16 Where Does Our Trash Go?
18 Litter at School
20 Keeping Water Clean
22 Looking After Ponds
24 Take Care of the Ocean Beaches
26 Clean Beaches
28 Litter in the Ocean
30 Glossary
31 Web Sites
32 Index

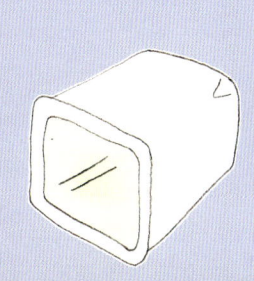

A Whole Lot of Litter

Nature has ways of dealing with things that are no longer wanted—such as dead leaves.

All trees lose their leaves every year and grow new ones. The old leaves fall to the ground where they slowly rot and become part of the soil. This helps to make the ground richer so new plants can grow.

When leaves change color and drop off the trees in the autumn, they become part of the leaf litter. This lies on the ground and rots.

But many of the things we no longer want do not rot like this. Plastic bags and bottles may lie around for hundreds of years. When we drop trash in the street or park, or throw it into the ocean, river, or lake it looks ugly. It can also kill wild animals and clog up waterways.

Litter Can Kill

The simplest things can be dangerous for animals.

- Curious hedgehogs often creep into empty yogurt containers. But they get stuck because of their spines and cannot get out again.

- Never throw the plastic soda can holders into an ocean, lake, or river. Diving birds and fish get caught in them and die. Small mammals can get trapped in them on land too.

- Water animals sometimes mistake floating plastic bags for food. But if they swallow them, they may choke and die.

- Waterbirds often become tangled up in fishing lines thrown away in the water.

One Small Fact

Look for a biodegradable label on packaging. This means it will rot away.

A Step in the Right Direction

You might think that what you do does not matter, but it matters very much. Every time you put a piece of litter into a trash can rather than dropping it on the ground, you take a step in the right direction. You can make a difference—everyone can. If lots of people take a small step in the right direction, these small steps will add up to one big step.

5

What Is Litter?

Litter is garbage that someone has dropped on the ground instead of putting it in a trash can.

Litter can be anything from a candy wrapper to an old sofa. Have you seen any today? You might see packaging from food, candy or chewing gum, soda cans, plastic bottles, pieces of paper, and bits of plastic. Do you or any of your friends drop litter?

One Small Fact
We throw away more than 251 million tons (228 t) of garbage in the United States each year.

More than 30 percent of the garbage and yard trimmings we throw away are recycled.

Dogs

No one wants to see dog waste on the sidewalks or in the park, so dog owners need to clean up after their pets. If your family has a dog, help your parents remember to bring some plastic bags or a poop scoop every time you take the dog for a walk.

If you feel like just dropping the food or candy wrapper on the ground—don't! Always remember that if you do drop litter it's not going to go away by itself. Someone else has to pick it up.

In most countries, it is a crime to drop litter in public places and you can be given a fine. These symbols remind people to put their litter in a trash container.

Litter in the Streets

If people see litter lying around, they are more likely to drop litter. If a street is clean, everyone is more likely to want to keep it clean.

Litter can be dangerous as well as ugly and dirty. And it can attract pests such as rats and cockroaches, which can spread disease.

Help keep your street and town clean by putting your litter in a trash can. And if a trash can is not handy or is full, take your litter home. Your litter is your responsibility.

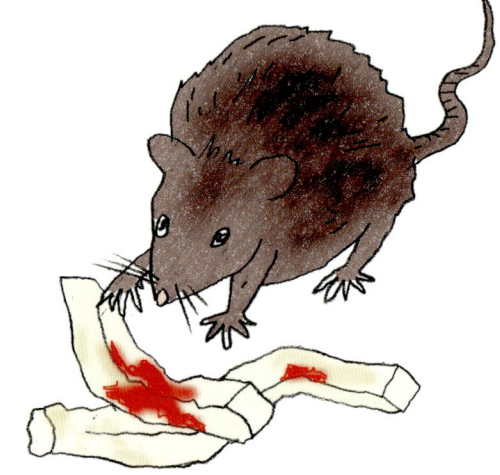

When people drop food litter in the street, pests such as rats and mice come and eat it.

Litter lies in the gutters of a street in Berlin, Germany, after a summer parade.

I Can Make a Difference

CLEAN UP DAY!

**Saturday, May 8
11:00**

Wear old clothes and come and help us clean up the playground

Everyone welcome

Bring gloves and trash bags

FREE SODA POP AND COOKIES FOR ALL VOLUNTEERS

It is amazing how quickly you can clear up litter when you have plenty of help.

How about getting together with your family and friends for a clean up day in your street or local playground? Be very careful and watch what you pick up. Always wear thick gloves and ask an adult if you think something you find might be dangerous.

One Small Fact

Lots of trash can be recycled. Plastic bottles can be melted down and made into new things such as fleece clothing, fences, and park benches.

Cleaning the Streets

Do you know how streets are cleaned and kept free from litter?

Local, state, and federal governments keep the streets and highways clean and take away trash. Street-sweeping trucks drive along slowly, brushing up trash from the gutter. They also collect fallen leaves and litter that can clog the drains.

This street sweeper has brushes that gather up litter from the streets of Boston, Massachusetts.

Workers in trash trucks empty containers and the special containers for dog waste. Street cleaners sweep the pavements and gutters and pick up smaller pieces of trash.

In some cities around the world, the streets are washed every morning. In Paris, sweeping machines spray the streets with water before anyone is up and about.

Gum Fact
A piece of gum costs 9 cents to buy and $1.50 to $3.00 to clean up.

Sticky Problem

One big problem for street cleaners is chewing gum dropped on the pavement. It is difficult to remove without special cleaning equipment. Some theme parks and airports do not sell gum to lessen this problem. So, if you chew gum—never drop it on the ground.

Adopt a Highway

Many places in the United States have a program called Adopt a Highway. Local groups and businesses adopt a stretch of road nearby and help to keep it clean and clear of any trash. In the state of California, more than half of the roads have been adopted. The program has been so successful that it is starting up in the United Kingdom too.

Packaging and Fast Food

How does packaging become a litter problem? One of the biggest causes of litter today is packaging and especially packaging for food.

Many foods are sold in plastic packaging, especially by supermarkets. Fruits and vegetables are often wrapped in plastic and so are lots of ready meals. Most sandwiches come in plastic or cardboard boxes, and beverages are sold in plastic bottles or aluminum cans. All this packaging is thrown away.

Fast-food restaurants sell food such as burgers and pizzas in plastic packaging, which some people drop in the street—along with any of the food they have not eaten. This creates litter and also attracts creatures such as rats, foxes, and birds who come to eat the leftover food.

Waste from fast-food restaurants is one of the major litter problems today.

Junk Mail

Junk mail adds to litter problems. Restaurants and other businesses print ads about their food or services. These ads are mailed or delivered to all the houses in the neighborhood. Some of these ads are recycled, but many are dropped in the streets and end up as litter.

I Can Make a Difference

Another major cause of litter is plastic bags. About 100 million plastic shopping bags are used each year in the United States. Many of these plastic bags end up as litter in streets and parks where they can be harmful to wildlife. Plastic bags take 400 to 1,000 years to decompose! Ask your family to take strong, reusable bags for shopping or buy cotton bags that will last for years.

One Small Fact

In 2005, 62 million trees were cut down to produce junk mail in the United States.

What Do We Throw Away at Home?

A lot of food packaging is thrown away at home, when the groceries are unpacked. What else does your family put out for the trash collector?

The garbage we throw away at home, such as leftover food, packaging, paper, cans, and bottles is called household waste. The trash that factories, shops, offices, and schools throw away is called industrial and commercial waste.

I Can Make a Difference

- Check out your family's trash. How many bags of trash did your household put out for the trash collector this week?

- Count how many plastic or glass bottles and cans your family recycled. How much paper or cardboard did you recycle?

- Is there anything else in the trash that you could reuse or recycle?

Some things we throw away can be dangerous. They can harm people, animals, and the world around us. Harmful trash includes things such as batteries, paint, and electrical equipment. We all need to be very careful about where and how we throw these things away.

An amazing amount of trash can be recycled. Paper, cans, and plastic and glass bottles can be recycled. Garden waste and grass clippings can be used for landfills. Trash collection businesses may provide separate containers for garden waste and other recyclable items. Some cities have recycling centers where you can take your separated trash for recycling.

Thousands of metal cans are crushed into huge cubes ready to be recycled.

Where Does Our Trash Go?

What happens to the trash we throw away at home or in the street?

In most U.S. cities, household trash is collected by special trucks every week. The trucks take the trash to garbage or landfill sites, where it is buried in the ground. Trash from public trash containers also goes to landfill sites.

One Small Fact

In 2006, each U.S. citizen threw away 4.6 pounds (2.1 kg) of trash each day.

At large landfill sites, machines like this tractor are used to shovel bags of trash.

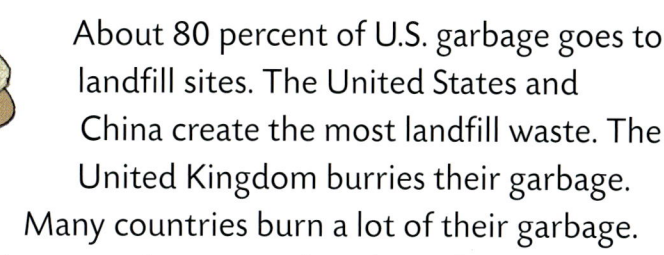

About 80 percent of U.S. garbage goes to landfill sites. The United States and China create the most landfill waste. The United Kingdom burries their garbage. Many countries burn a lot of their garbage. For example, Denmark and Sweden burn more than half the garbage they produce.

If your parents want to throw away something big, such as a sofa, a television, or a washing machine, they pay to have it taken away or take it to the local landfill themselves. Even big things like this can sometimes be recycled. If your family has a computer, you can find Web sites that accept things you no longer need (and to find things other people might be giving away). This helps to keep a lot of useful trash out of the landfills.

Dumped Cars

Some people dump old cars, tires, car batteries, and even boats on the side of a road. This adds up to tons of trash. It is unsightly and can harm the land and the wildlife.

Litter at School

Is there litter in your school? What could you do to make it cleaner?

In some Japanese schools, the students have to do all the cleaning. It is amazing—when people have to pick up litter they think twice about dropping it. You could get together with some friends and check on what kinds of litter are dropped in your school and which areas have the most litter.

I Can Make a Difference

If you do something about litter, other people might follow you and do the same. You could do a litter survey in your school. Make a form like this one and fill it in every day for a week.

Date: Name of school: Surveyed by:

TYPE OF LITTER	PLACE FOUND					
	Classroom	Playground	Sports Field	Hallways	Bathrooms	Gym
Snack packets		IIII I	II		I	
Food	I	IIII IIII I				II
Paper	II		IIII			
Drink cans/bottles	IIII II	IIII IIII II	IIII I	IIII	I	
Plastic bags	II	IIII	II			II
Chewing gum					IIII	IIII I
Other litter	IIII I	IIII IIII		I	III	

Everyone can help make sure that the school playground is kept free of litter.

What Next?

Look at all the survey forms to see what and where the worst problems are. Can you think of ways to cut down on litter? Here are some ideas.

- Make some posters asking people to use the trash containers more.

- Ask the school to put trash containers in places where you found lots of litter.

- Find out if the trash containers can be emptied more often.

- Take turns to check the playground and other areas.

One Small Fact

Removing litter and cleaning the streets costs California $28 million a year.

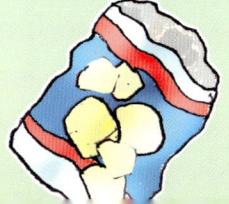

19

Keeping Water Clean

Dirty or polluted water also causes problems in the world today.

There is a lot of water on Earth. But most of the water is in the ocean. This water is salty, so we cannot drink it or use it to grow things. Much of the fresh water on Earth is frozen solid at the North and South Poles. You can see where these are on the maps below.

The freshwater that we use comes from rain and snow that collects in rivers and lakes. When this water is dirty or polluted, it can kill wild animals and can make people ill if they drink it.

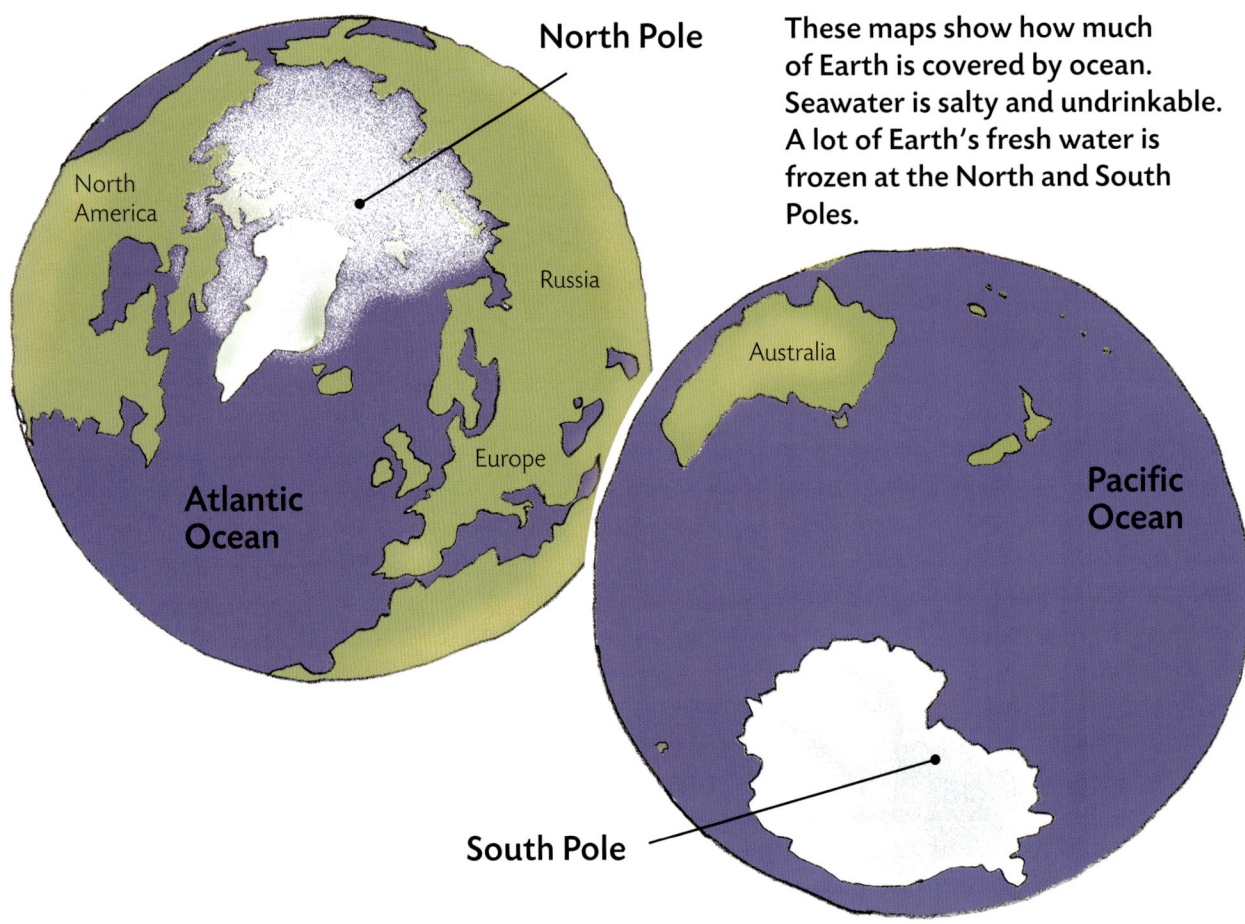

These maps show how much of Earth is covered by ocean. Seawater is salty and undrinkable. A lot of Earth's fresh water is frozen at the North and South Poles.

The water in Millstätter Lake in southern Austria is sparkling clear.

The water around Bonny Island in Nigeria has been polluted by trash.

What Makes Water Dirty?

Many different things can make water dirty or polluted. Here are some of the most important.

- Litter and trash thrown into the water.

- Oil and chemicals spilled on roads. When it rains, the rain washes the chemicals into rivers and streams.

- Chemicals that farmers put on their fields. Rain washes them off the fields and into streams and rivers.

- Chemicals thrown away by factories can kill fish and other wildlife.

- Plastic fishing lines used by fishermen.

21

Looking After Ponds

Lots of plants and animals live in watery places, from tiny ponds to huge lakes. Do you have a pond in your yard or neighborhood?

Did you know that there are more than a thousand different animals that live in and around ponds? You might see frogs, toads or newts, water birds, voles, shrews, and snails. Keeping ponds clean helps the animals—litter can hurt them and make the water dirty and difficult to live in.

One Small Fact
Ponds help support tadpoles, ducks, and raccoons.

22

I Can Make a Difference

Ask your parents to help you find out whether there is a pond in your nearest wild area. There may be a local group you can join that looks after wild areas, ponds, and streams. Or ask your teacher if you can arrange a cleanup day. You could even keep a journal of the animals you see at the pond through the seasons.

Take Care
NEVER try to clean up a pond by yourself. Always wear thick gloves when you pick up litter.

Even the smallest pond may be home to frogs, toads, and newts.

Take Care of the Ocean Beaches

Have you been to the ocean beaches? Did you see any litter there? Many beaches are dirty and littered with trash.

You may see lots of bits of plastic, such as bags and water bottles, on the beach. Plastic items do not rot away naturally. That means they remain as litter for hundreds of years after we throw them away.

Plastic trash makes beaches look ugly. But it can also hurt all sorts of wild animals. Ocean birds sometimes swallow pieces of plastic and die. Fish and other ocean animals can get tangled up in plastic fishing lines or nets.

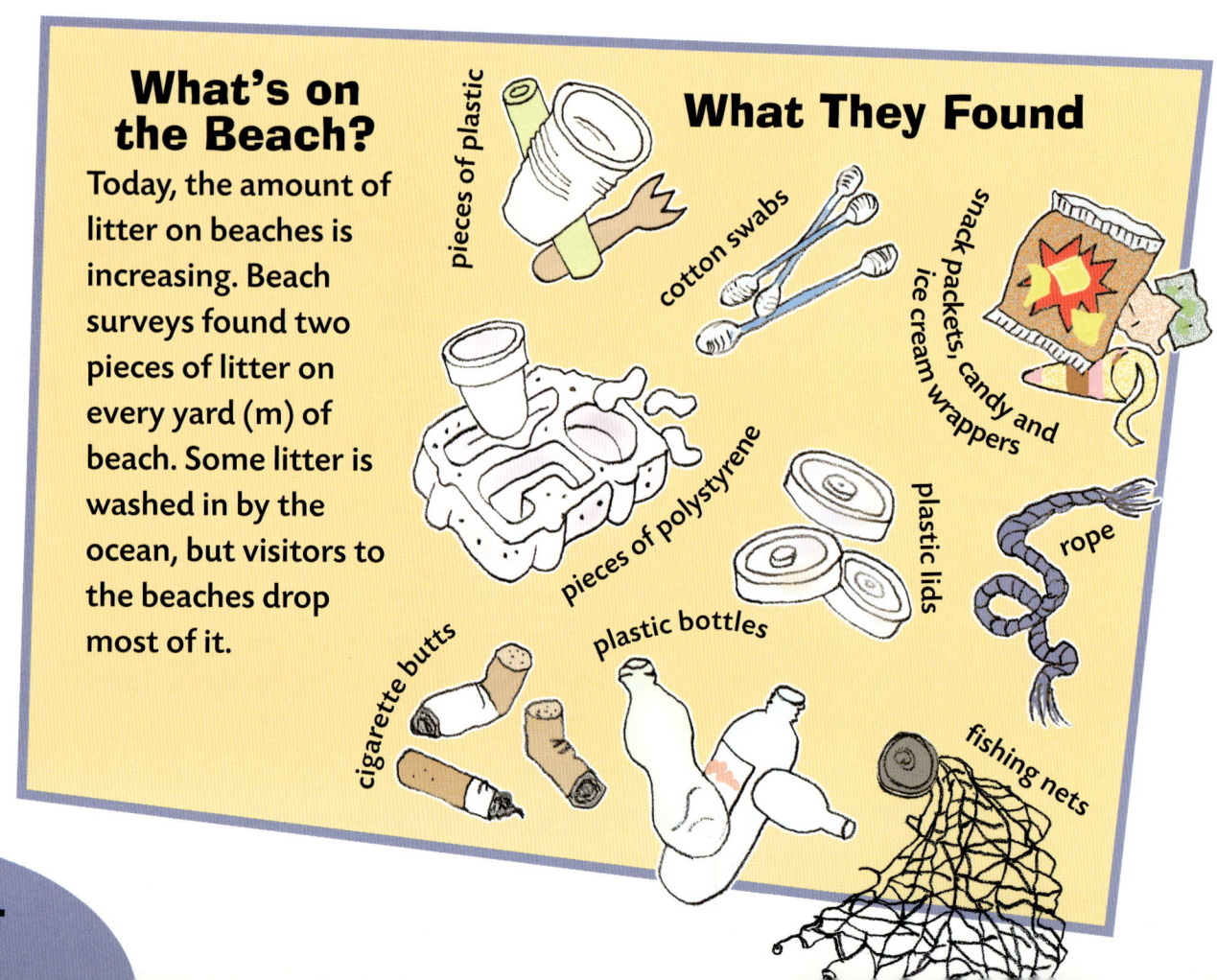

What's on the Beach?

Today, the amount of litter on beaches is increasing. Beach surveys found two pieces of litter on every yard (m) of beach. Some litter is washed in by the ocean, but visitors to the beaches drop most of it.

What They Found

pieces of plastic, cotton swabs, snack packets, candy and ice cream wrappers, pieces of polystyrene, plastic lids, rope, cigarette butts, plastic bottles, fishing nets

This beach on the Spanish island of Mallorca is polluted with trash.

I Can Make a Difference

If you live near the ocean, find out if any beach cleanups are planned. You could go along to help. If no one is looking after your nearest beach, ask your parents if you can get together with some friends and plan some cleanups.

Clean Beaches

Have you heard of the Blue Flag and Blue Wave programs? These help to make sure that beaches are clean and the water is good for swimming.

A Blue Flag or Blue Wave beach has to be well looked after. There are information boards for visitors about the beach and how clean the water is. Every beach must have trash and recycling containers. There must be special equipment for lifesaving and first aid. They should also have restrooms and a supply of fresh water that is safe for visitors to drink.

Blue Flag and Blue Wave

The Blue Flag program started in France in 1985. The flag has been given to more than 3,000 beaches and marinas around the world since. A Blue Flag is given to a beach for just one year and then it is evaluated again. The Blue Wave program does the same thing in the United States. It was started in 1998 by the Clean Beaches Council.

I Can Make a Difference

Next time you go to a beach with your family or friends, make sure you take a bag to put your trash in. If the beach has trash and recycling containers, leave your litter there. If not, bring it home with you and put it in your trash or recycling container.

Litter in the Ocean

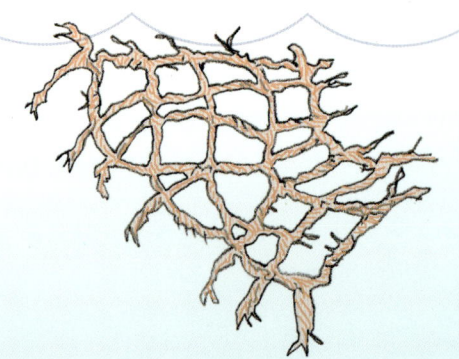

Litter in the ocean often hurts wild animals. There is a huge amount of litter in the seas and oceans around the world.

A huge patch of trash is floating in the middle of the Pacific Ocean. It is twice the size of Texas and is mostly made up of plastic litter.

People visiting beaches drop a lot of the litter and it gets washed into the ocean. People on boats also drop litter overboard instead of taking it back to the harbor to throw away.

When people throw litter into the ocean, they are dropping their trash into the home of sea animals.

A million ocean birds and 100,000 ocean animals die every year because they become tangled up in old fishing lines and nets or because they swallow plastic.

Floating plastic bags in the oceans kill many sea creatures.

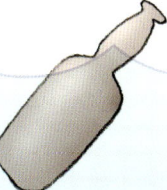

A boat collecting trash from the Mediterranean sea off the south coast of France.

Marine turtles are now an endangered species because of threats to them from fishing lines, nets, and plastic waste.

I Can Make a Difference

Every September, a group called Clean Up the World (visit Web site on page 31) organizes a Clean Up the World Weekend. People around the world think of ways they can clean up the place where they live and make it better to live in. Why not find out if you can help?

29

Glossary

biodegradable
Biodegradable garbage will rot away after a while. Fruit and grass cuttings are biodegradable. Non-biodegradable trash, such as cans and plastic, will never rot.

cockroaches
Large insects, some of which feed on food waste.

endangered
An endangered animal or plant is one that is at risk of becoming extinct—disappearing from Earth altogether. This may be because it has lost its habitat or food source or because many have been killed or destroyed.

fast food
Food which is prepared and served very quickly after you order it, for example, pizza or burgers and fries.

junk mail
Letters sent through the mail or ads put in your mailbox or door to encourage you to buy something or visit a restaurant.

landfill sites
Places where garbage is dumped and usually buried.

packaging
The wrapping around something.

pests
Insects or small animals that damage plants or food supplies and may carry diseases.

polluted
Water, land, or air that is dirty or dangerous to use or live in.

recycling
Using things again. Many items and materials can be reused, from paper to mobile phones.

Web Sites

http://www.cleanuptheworld.org/en/
Nations across the world work toward cleaning up our environment.

http://earth911.org/
The Earth 911 Web site offers information on recycling and activities.

http://www.epa.gov/kids/
This U.S. Environmental Protection Agency Web site has activities and games on trash and recycling.

http://www.keepoceansclean.org/home/
Play games and learn how to keep the ocean clean.

http://www.litteritcostsyou.org/schools.aspx
Be part of the litter solution! Games, activities, and programs get you involved in cleaning up the litter problem.

http://www.nmfs.noaa.gov/habitat/
Learn how to conserve and manage marine resources.

Index

animals 5, 12, 13, 15, 20, 22, 23, 24, 28, 29

beaches 24–25, 26–27, 28
bottles 5, 6, 9, 12, 14, 15, 18, 24

cans 5, 6, 12, 14, 15, 18
cars 17
chewing gum 6, 11, 18
cleanup days 9, 23, 25

dog waste 7, 11

electrical equipment 15

fishing lines and nets 5, 21, 24, 28, 29
food 5, 6, 7, 8, 12, 13, 14, 18

junk mail 13, 30

landfill sites 16, 17, 30
leaves 4, 10

Pacific Ocean 28
packaging 5, 6, 12, 14, 30
pests 8, 30
plastic bags 5, 7, 13, 18, 24, 28
plastic litter 5, 6, 9, 12, 13, 14, 15, 21, 24, 28, 29
Poles 20
ponds 22–23

recycling 14, 15, 17, 26, 27, 30

schools 14, 18–19
street cleaning 8, 10–11

trash cans 5, 6, 7, 8, 9, 11, 15, 16, 26

water 20–21, 22–23
water pollution 20, 21, 22